Dear Parent:
Your child's love of reading starts here!

Every child learns to read in a different way and at his or her own speed. Some go back and forth between reading levels and read favorite books again and again. Others read through each level in order. You can help your young reader improve and become more confident by encouraging his or her own interests and abilities. From books your child reads with you to the first books he or she reads alone, there are I Can Read Books for every stage of reading:

SHARED READING
Basic language, word repetition, and whimsical illustrations, ideal for sharing with your emergent reader

BEGINNING READING
Short sentences, familiar words, and simple concepts for children eager to read on their own

READING WITH HELP
Engaging stories, longer sentences, and language play for developing readers

READING ALONE
Complex plots, challenging vocabulary, and high-interest topics for the independent reader

ADVANCED READING
Short paragraphs, chapters, and exciting themes for the perfect bridge to chapter books

I Can Read Books have introduced children to the joy of reading since 1957. Featuring award-winning authors and illustrators and a fabulous cast of beloved characters, I Can Read Books set the standard for beginning readers.

A lifetime of discovery begins with the magical words **"I Can Read!"**

Visit www.icanread.com for information
on enriching your child's reading experience.

ISBN 978-0-545-66023-5

12 11 10 9 8   15 16 17 18/0

Printed in the U.S.A.   40

First Scholastic printing, October 2013

FLAT STANLEY

Goes Camping

created by Jeff Brown
by Lori Haskins Houran
pictures by Macky Pamintuan

SCHOLASTIC INC.

Stanley Lambchop lived
with his mother,
his father,
and his little brother, Arthur.

Stanley was four feet tall,

about a foot wide,

and half an inch thick.

He had been flat ever since

a bulletin board fell on him.

There were lots of good things about being flat.

Stanley could put on sunscreen in one swipe.

Stanley had the best back float
at the pool.

Stanley had

the loudest belly flop, too.

But sometimes it was hard

being the only flat kid in town.

"I'm sick of being flat,"
said Stanley one morning.
"Flat is lame."
"Lame?" said Mrs. Lambchop.
"Why, some of the best things
in the world are flat!"

"Like the newspaper,"

said Mr. Lambchop.

"And fried eggs. And pancakes.

And bacon," said Arthur.

"I guess so," said Stanley.

After breakfast Mr. Lambchop
started loading up the car
with tents and sleeping bags.

"What's going on?" asked Arthur.

"We're going camping," said Mrs. Lambchop.

"This family needs some fresh air."

"All right!" yelled Arthur.

Stanley barely smiled.

After a short drive, the Lambchops arrived
at the Roarin' River Campground.
Stanley was helpful, as usual.
He helped carry firewood.

Stanley blocked the wind

so his mother could start a fire.

But Stanley just wasn't himself.

He wouldn't even eat any s'mores.

"Too flat," he muttered.

"Why don't you two go exploring?"
suggested Mr. Lambchop.
"Good idea," said Mrs. Lambchop.
"Just don't get lost
or fall off a cliff
or touch any poison ivy.
Have fun, dears!"

Stanley and Arthur set out.

"Hey, animal tracks!" said Arthur.

"Let's follow them!"

The boys followed the tracks

along the river, through some trees,

and up a steep hill

with a cliff on one side.

"The tracks end here," said Arthur.

He peered over the cliff.

"I wonder what kind of animal

made them."

"Um, Arthur," said Stanley.

Arthur turned around.

"Skunk!" he whispered.

"Let's get out of here!"

But the boys were trapped.

The skunk was on one side.

The cliff was on the other.

Then the skunk raised its tail!

"What do we do?" Arthur wailed.

"Mom said not to fall off a cliff,"
said Stanley.

"She didn't say not to jump off."

Suddenly Stanley grabbed Arthur
by both hands and jumped!
"AAAAAAAAAAAAHHHHH!"
Arthur screamed.

Then Arthur opened his eyes.

He wasn't falling.

He was sailing!

Above him, Stanley's body

made the perfect parachute.

The boys landed with a gentle PLOP.

"That was awesome!" said Arthur.

"Thanks," said Stanley.

"Now, where are we?"

Arthur and Stanley looked around.

All they saw were trees.

"We're lost!" said Arthur.

"And it's getting dark!"

Then Stanley spotted something.

"There's the river!" he said.

"Our campground is on the river!"

The boys ran to the water's edge.

About a mile downstream

were two cozy Lambchop tents!

"What can we do?

It will be dark before we can walk

that far," said Arthur.

"I know!" said Stanley.

Stanley got a running start

and belly flopped into the river.

SPLASH!

Then he flipped over onto his back.

"Climb on!"

"Woohoo!" cried Arthur.

"I always wanted to go rafting!"

Arthur and Stanley made it
back to camp, drippy but safe.
"Let's keep this to ourselves,"
said Stanley.
"I can't believe we got lost
AND went off a cliff," Arthur said.
"At least we didn't
touch poison ivy!"

"There you are!" said Mrs. Lambchop.

"Just in time for supper."

That night, Arthur whispered

to Stanley from his sleeping bag,

"You know, if you weren't flat,

you couldn't have saved us today."

Stanley smiled.

"Maybe being flat isn't so lame,"

he said.

And the next day, Stanley found out

another good thing about being flat.

He could put on poison ivy cream
in one swipe.